To the little people in my life: Meg, Justin, Emma, Philippa,
Dagny, Teancum, Cumeni, Jershon, Bronte, Thane, Mica,
Brooke, Abigail, Joseph, Eliza, Eli, Nathan, and Isaac. —J.N.H.

For little Katrina. —D.A.

STERLING and the distinctive Sterling logo are registered
trademarks of Sterling Publishing Co., Inc.

Library of Congress Cataloging-in-Publication Data

Hulme, Joy N.
 Easter babies : a Springtime counting book / by Joy N. Hulme ;
illustrated by Dan Andreasen.
  p. cm.
 Summary: Presents numbers from one to twelve in illustrations of baby animals on a farm,
children playing on a playground, and church bells ringing to welcome spring.
 ISBN 978-1-4027-6352-6 (alk. paper)
 [1. Stories in rhyme. 2. Animals--Infancy--Fiction. 3. Farm life--Fiction. 4. Spring--Fiction.
5. Easter--Fiction. 6. Counting.] I. Andreasen, Dan, ill. II. Title.
 PZ8.3.H878Sp 2010
 [E]--dc22

2008047126

Lot#:
4 6 8 10 9 7 5 3
11/09

Published by Sterling Publishing Co., Inc.
387 Park Avenue South, New York, NY 10016
Text © 2010 by Joy N. Hulme
Illustrations © 2010 by Dan Andreasen
Distributed in Canada by Sterling Publishing
c/o Canadian Manda Group, 165 Dufferin Street
Toronto, Ontario, Canada M6K 3H6
Distributed in the United Kingdom by GMC Distribution Services
Castle Place, 166 High Street, Lewes, East Sussex, England BN7 1XU
Distributed in Australia by Capricorn Link (Australia) Pty. Ltd.
P.O. Box 704, Windsor, NSW 2756, Australia

Printed in China

Sterling ISBN 978-1-4027-6352-6

For information about custom editions, special sales, premium and
corporate purchases, please contact Sterling Special Sales
Department at 800-805-5489 or specialsales@sterlingpublishing.com.

The illustrations in this book were created using
a combination of digital art and traditional oil paint.

Designed by Chrissy Kwasnik.

EASTER BABIES

A SPRINGTIME COUNTING BOOK

WRITTEN BY
Joy N. Hulme

ILLUSTRATED BY
Dan Andreasen

STERLING

New York / London

When signs of spring are in the air,
we look for babies everywhere!

1 newborn foal gets to his feet
to walk on wobbly legs.

2 brooding hens sit quite content
to hatch their nests of eggs.

3 playful kids will jump the fence and get in lots of trouble.

4 bunnies looking just alike
are each the other's double.

5 nestlings with wide open bills
are screeching to be fed.

6 cheeping chicks peck up their food,
each with a bobbing head.

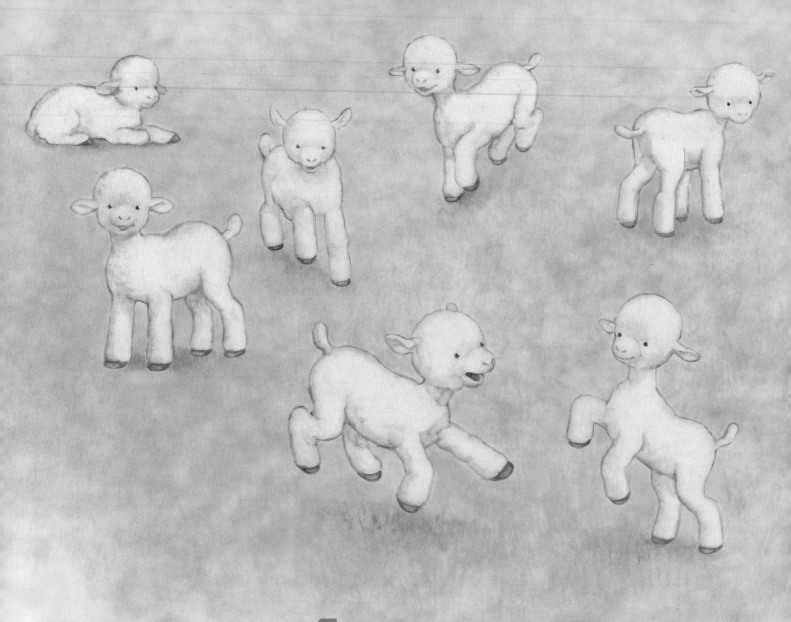

In grassy meadows 7 lambs
frolic on frisky feet.

8 piglets wiggle near the sow
to find a place to eat.

9 kittens with their eyes still shut
nuzzle close together.

10 ducklings paddle in the stream
no matter what the weather.

11 children in the park
are racing, chasing, swinging.

In churches all around the town
12 Easter bells are ringing . . .

. . . to celebrate the signs that spring
has brought new life to everything.